LEGENDS
(in their own lunchbox)

Lucy: The Boss

Paul Collins & Christian Bocquée

capstone
classroom

capstone
classroom

Legends (in Their Own Lunchbox) is published by Capstone Classroom
1710 Roe Crest Drive
North Mankato, MN 56003
www.capstoneclassroom.com

Library of Congress Cataloging-In-Publication data is available on the Library of
Congress website.

ISBN: 978-1-4966-0254-1

This edition of *Lucy: The Boss* is published by arrangement with Macmillan Publishers
Australia Pty Ltd 2013.

Photo credits: iStockphoto.com/marlanu, **52**

This book has been officially leveled by using the F&P Text Level Gradient™
Leveling System.

Printed in China

Contents

MEET the Characters

I'm Lucy. I think everyone should do things my way. Kie-yah!

I'm Max, Lucy's best friend.

I'm Sean,
Lucy's other
best friend.

I'm Miss Brussels.
I don't put up
with any nonsense.
Especially from
Lucy Lee!

Chapter 1
Sprung!

Lucy, Sean, and Max were in their favorite place in the entire school — the cafeteria.

"Fries, please," Lucy said.

"We're out of fries. Next!" snapped Mrs. Barge.

"Wait a minute," said Lucy. "You can't be out of fries!"

"Well, we are," said Mrs. Barge.

"Can't you fry some more?" said Sean. Several other kids joined in. "Yeah! More!"

Mrs. Barge glared at them. "There are no more fries," she snapped. "And no pizza, either! Nothing fatty, greasy, yucky, or fattening!"

"I'll have a hot dog," said Lucy angrily.

"They're both yucky *and* fattening," Mrs. Barge said. "We only have healthy food now, like lettuce, tomato — all the salad you can eat."

"Rabbit food!" Lucy said. She stomped over to a table and sat down.

Sean and Max joined her. "What
are we going to *eat*?" said Sean. His
stomach rumbled. "I'm starving!"

"I've got some sandwiches," said Max.

They sat munching old peanut butter
sandwiches.

"They taste like cardboard," said Lucy.

Max eyed his sandwich. "So would you if you'd been in my bag for two weeks."

"We're all going to starve," Lucy said. She closed her eyes. "Only my training in the ancient art of Tai Chi will save me."

"What about us?" asked Max.

"Well, there's nothing we can do about it," said Sean, picking crumbs off the table. "It's not Mrs. Barge's fault the school wants to go healthy."

Lucy crossed her arms and huffed loudly. She didn't notice that Principal Newbury was standing just behind her. "If I were in charge of this school, I'd see that everything worked properly."

"Would you now?" asked Principal Newbury.

Lucy jumped but recovered quickly. "Yes!" she said.

The loudspeakers came on at lunchtime.

"Good afternoon, students," came Principal Newbury's voice. "I have some news. I'm going away for a week. And I've decided to leave a student in charge. This student will be acting as principal for the whole school!"

There was an amazed silence.

"And that student will be — Lucy Lee!"

Chapter 2
Day One:
Overjoyed

"Hi, Lucy!"

"Good morning, Lucy!"

"Lucy, can I have your autograph?"

Lucy signed several notebooks that first morning. She also signed three casts (two legs, one arm), half a dozen sweaty

palms and one piece of
(unused!) toilet paper.

She refused to sign three
pairs of stinky socks.

A chalk drawing of Lucy appeared on the gym wall. Lucy even sat in Principal Newbury's shiny leather chair.

"How do I look?" she asked Sean and Max.

"Cool," said Sean.

"Scary," said Max.

"Okay, the first thing we do is order good food for the cafeteria, and we'll have free fries for everyone ..."

Lucy worked very hard all that day solving problems and listening to students' concerns. She even listened to the teachers.

Lucy visited the cafeteria. Everyone had enough to eat and was happy — except for Mrs. Barge.

On her way back to her office Lucy
ran into Miss Brussels, the meanest
teacher in the entire school. It was like
running into a brick wall.

"*Ouch!*" said Lucy, rubbing her nose.

"I need money for the hockey team," said Miss Brussels.

"I don't like hockey," said Lucy.

"I don't care what you like, young missy, we have to play Fenton Junior on Friday and we need a bus."

Lucy's eyes narrowed. "I'm canceling the hockey team. You can play ping-pong instead!"

"We could play chess, too," Miss Brussels said. "We could play Scrabble. BUT WE'RE A HOCKEY TEAM!"

Lucy was blown backward by the shouting. Were it not for her superb martial arts balance, she would have been knocked off her feet.

But she simply marched off with her
nose in the air.

"*Kie-YAH!*" Lucy screamed,
chopping an imaginary opponent.
"*Eeeeee!*"

Chapter 3
Day Two: Overboard

Everybody wanted something! More money, more books, more chairs, more room, more detention. (And less detention.)

And Lucy saw that someone had drawn a HUGE red X over her wall painting!!

Lucy offered a big reward. Nobody
was going to make fun of *her*.

"Put up these posters," she told Sean and Max. Lucy was in a really bad mood now.

She saw a girl throw a piece of paper on the floor. "Detention!" she yelled. She had Sean draw up a new rule:

Then she tripped on something.
Three boys giggled.

"DETENTION!" she screamed at them. "Ha! You're not laughing now!"

So another rule went up:

She saw Jenny Jinks picking her nose. Yuck!

By the end of the day, Lucy had added thirty-seven new rules. She felt much better now.

Chapter 4
Day Three: Overwhelmed

"I want them expelled!" Lucy shouted.

Sean was taking notes. "How do you spell 'expelled?'" he asked.

"Buy a dictionary!" snapped Lucy. "Hi-YAH!" she yelled, karate-chopping the table. And now her hand hurt.

"What's that noise?"

There was a rumbling, thunder-like sound in the distance. "The students are having a meeting," said Max.

Lucy jumped up. "A meeting? Why didn't anyone tell me? They can't have a meeting unless I say so! I'm the acting principal of this school! Make me a sign, Sean. NO MORE MEETINGS WITHOUT PERMISSION FROM THE ACTING PRINCIPAL!"

Sean got to work.

Max said, "Miss Brussels is setting them up."

"See?" said Lucy. "She's trying to destroy me. Just because she hates ping-pong."

"I bet she wants my job," she added.
"Well, I won't let her have it!"

"What are you going to do?"

"Fire her!" said Lucy. "For — for trying
to overthrow the acting principal!"

So Miss Brussels was fired.

But she didn't go without a fight.
She called one last meeting and spoke to
the other teachers. She spoke very well.
She sobbed and cried.

Before long every teacher at the
meeting was crying and sobbing, too.

At the end of Miss Brussels's performance, every teacher walked out of the school.

• ● •

"WHAT DO YOU MEAN THE TEACHERS LEFT?" Lucy screamed. "The bell hasn't rung! And who's going to teach the students?"

Neither Sean nor Max had any ideas.

Lucy buried her face in her hands. It was all going wrong and, worse still, everyone seemed to dislike her.

"We'd better check on the students," said Lucy.

The hallway outside the office looked like a war zone.

Books, paper planes, soda cans, and candy wrappers littered the floor.

One small boy was wriggling down the hallway. He'd been wrapped up like a mummy in toilet paper.

"Detention!" snapped Lucy as she walked past him. "No wriggling in the hallways."

"But — but —" stuttered the boy.

"Double detention," said Lucy. "For but-butting!"

Lucy poked her head into several classrooms. But nobody was learning anything — they were all having *fun*.

Lucy gave them the death stare.

"New rule!" said Lucy to Sean, who was following her, busily scribbling.

A wall of noise hit them when they arrived at the cafeteria. Lucy's legs went weak. All she could say was, "Oh. No. Oh. No."

At least half the school was there and they were having the biggest food fight ever!

Lucy cupped her mouth. "I want this to stop right NOW!" she yelled.

"That's her!" someone shouted.

"Get her!"

WHOOSH! WHOOSH! WHOOSH!

A dozen pies shot through the air.

Lucy leapt high and kicked two tarts out of the way.

"Eiyyy-YAH!"

She chopped two into mushy pulp.

"Kie-AI!"

She crouched and jumped.

"Hie-YAH!"

Pies splattered everywhere. But not even Lucy's stunning display of martial arts could save her and her friends.

Chapter 5
Day Four:
Overthrown

Lucy, Sean, and Max ran for their lives as an angry horde of students chased them.

"Get to the office!" yelled Lucy. "I'll hold them off at the door!"

Pies and donuts bombarded them and

a roll of toilet paper streamed down the hallway.

"Detention!" shouted acting principal Lucy Lee. "Wasting government property!"

"They're gaining on us!" wailed Sean.

Lucy didn't think they would make it to the office in time.

But worse was about to come. They dashed up a hallway and skidded around the last corner. Standing between them and the office was a grinning Miss Brussels.

Lucy's heart skipped a beat. Nobody had *ever* seen Miss Brussels grin.

"Hi there, Lucy, *boys*," said the former teacher.

"We're done for," said Sean, covering his face.

"No we're not," hissed Lucy. "Remember the math test last year?"

Max's eyes danced. "Yes!"

Sean peeked out between his fingers. "You mean when she — ?"

"YES!" said Max and Lucy together.

They ran toward Miss Brussels.
At the last minute they dropped onto all fours.

And *squeaked* and *scrabbled* around like little mice.

"Eeee, eee, eee, eee!" they chittered.

"Arrghhh!" Miss Brussels grabbed her skirt and ran screaming.

Lucy jumped up and chopped the air with her hands at Miss Brussels' back. "Ei-YAH!" she screamed.

Max and Sean grabbed and pulled Lucy into the office just in time. Sean locked the door.

"You're a genius!" said Max. "I forgot she's scared of mice!"

The students reached the office. They started kicking and thumping the door, chanting, "DOWN WITH LUCY LEE!"

Lucy went pale. "We're trapped. I *could* fight them off with my crouching tiger form," she said. She half closed her eyes and lifted her foot like a stork. Her hands wove the air like gliding doves and she slid into a crouch, like a tiger about to spring.

"We don't have time!" Max cried as the door shook.

"Why are they so mad?" asked Sean.

Lucy stood up. "It's my fault," she said. "I was an idiot. I thought I could improve things but I just made them worse. I never want to be boss of anything ever again!"

"Being the boss is never easy," said a voice.

The children gasped.

Principal Newbury stepped out of the shadows. She sat down in her chair. "Open the door, please, Lucy."

Lucy's eyes went wide. "But — but —!"

"Lucy?"

Lucy gulped and obediently opened

the door. The whole hallway went quiet. Not a single pie or donut was thrown.

"Everyone will please return to their classrooms," Mrs. Newbury said. "The experiment Lucy and I held is now over. Thank you all for joining in. Back to your classrooms, please. You too, Lucy, boys."

Lucy let out her breath. "Thanks, Principal Newbury," she said. "I think I've learned my lesson."

Mrs. Newbury beamed. "We're here to teach," she said.

Hmmm, thought Lucy as she headed off down the hallway. *Next time I'll do things a whole lot differently! For a start, I'll ban pie and donuts.*

Well, maybe not the donuts …

Lucy's Email

From: kung-fu-queen@litols.com
To: karatekid@litols.com
Sent: Sunday, October 16
Subject: My New Job

Hi Lily,

You'll never guess what happened to me last week. Mrs. Newbury made me the acting principal of my school! I had to keep making all these new rules — and all the kids kept breaking them. Miss Brussels even staged a walk-out on me! Guess being the boss isn't as easy as I thought.

Here's a picture of the guys and me pretending to be mice!

C-YA
Lucy

MORE LEGENDS!

Want to find out my
next high-kicking
adventure?
Read my next
book! Here's
what happens…

Lucy's been
employed as a
kung-fu bodyguard,
to protect her
friends from bullies.
But is it Lucy's high
kicks that scare
off the bullies?
Or something else?

Meet the Author

Paul Collins grew up dreaming of being famous. He joined a stunt team, became a commando, trained hard for two black belts in taekwondo and jujitsu, and became a kickboxer — but none of these led to fame. So now he writes about Lucy Lee. And she *is* famous. At least in her own lunchbox. Find out more about Paul at www.paulcollins.com.au.

Meet the Illustrator

Christian Bocquée grew up in Queensland, Australia. Some of that time he lived on a farm, far away from the hustle and bustle. From a young age he loved to draw his favorite things, like dinosaurs and knights in armor. He now lives in beautiful Brisbane. Sometimes he likes to take his sketchpad in hand and set off on drawing adventures. Find out more about Christian at www.christianbocquee.com.

Read all the books in Set 2